BEGINNINGS

BEGINNINGS

How Families Come to Be

Virginia Kroll
illustrated by Stacey Schuett

Albert Whitman & Company
Morton Grove, Illinois

Text © 1994 by Virginia L. Kroll.
Illustrations © 1994 by Stacey Schuett.
Published in 1994 by Albert Whitman & Company,
6340 Oakton St., Morton Grove, Illinois 60053-2723.
Published simultaneously in Canada by General Publishing, Limited, Toronto.
Printed in the U.S.A.
10 9 8 7 6 5 4 3 2 1

Designer: Sandy Newell.
Text typeface: New Century Schoolbook.
Illustration media: Acrylic and pastel.

Library of Congress Cataloging-in-Publication Data
Kroll, Virginia L.
Beginnings : how families come to be / Virginia L. Kroll ;
illustrated by Stacey Schuett.
p. cm.
Summary: Parents and children discuss how their families came to be, covering birth
families and various kinds of adoptive families.
ISBN 0-8075-0602-8
[1. Adoption–Fiction. 2. Families–Fiction.]
I. Schuett, Stacey, ill. II. Title.
PZ7.K9227Be 1994   93-29594
[E]–dc20   CIP
                                                                                   AC

For Maureen, who loved enough to let go.
V.L.K.

For Hannah, Sibylle, and Andy.
S.S.

*T*ell me, Mommy, about how I began."

"Daddy and I were full of love. After we were married for a while, I became pregnant, and I was full of you! You grew inside, giving me a basketball belly. And just when I looked like I could really bounce, you came right out of me, kicking and squawling, wrinkled and bawling, the most beautiful thing I ever did see! Daddy and I sputtered and sparkled with joy."

"Like fireworks?"

"Even brighter. We told the world with letters and wore out the phone. 'It's a boy!' we cried over and over, and it was new each time we said it.

"Daddy handed out blue bubble gum cigars at work and put up a bouquet of balloons on the porch rail the day we brought you home from the hospital. We named you Ruben because it means 'Behold, a son.'"

"And we're a family, forever and ever."

"Forever and ever. A family."

"Tell me, Mama, the story of me."

"Our hearts, Daddy's and mine, each had an empty place that only a child could fill, so we set out to find you. First we made a call to FIA."

"That stands for 'Families Interested in Adoption.'"

"Yes, it does. They put us in touch with an adoption worker. We made a hundred more phone calls, answered a million questions—"

"and filled out a zillion papers."

"But we didn't mind. Because in time, our agency worker called to say that a little girl had been born. Her mother couldn't take care of her, and she wanted her to have parents who could."

"So a silver plane carried me halfway around the world."
"Yes, over fields where farmers were picking crops, over boats where fishermen netted fish from the sea."

"And you waited a long time."

"Oh, the waiting seemed like forever. We wore out a path in the airport floor. Finally, your plane touched down. There you were, pink and rosy, asleep and cozy in your chaperone's arms."

"I didn't wake up?"

"Wait. That part is coming.

"Your Korean name was Mee Kyong, which means 'Beauty and Brightness.' We silently thanked your other mother who had named you for what she knew you'd become. We thought it might be easier for you to have an American name when you came to live in America. So we named you after both your new American grandmothers.

"I whispered, 'Katherine Grace,' and that was the moment you opened your eyes and saw me. Daddy touched your hand, and you gripped his finger tightly."

"Did your empty places get filled up, Mama?"

"Right to the brim, and overflowing ever since."

"And now you're going to get a brother for me, all the way from South America. Give this to him, OK?"

"But honey, that's Ollie Orangutan, your favorite stuffed toy. Are you sure?"

"I'm sure. And when he gets here, Mama, can I tell him the story of how we got to be brother and sister?"

"Certainly, Katherine Grace. Right from the beginning."

Daddy, when I was first born, you were just my Uncle Joe, right?"

"Yes, until you were four months old."

"I couldn't talk yet, could I?"

"No, but you could smile, a big, beautiful, toothless grin, and your whole body smiled when your mouth did. That was the last thing your mommy—my sister—saw before she died. It made her very happy."

"And you adopted me right after that because you promised, right?"

"Because I wanted you and I promised, right. Your mommy wasn't married, and she was very sick. She wanted to make sure you stayed in our family, so she asked me if I'd raise you like my own. I said yes, of course I would."

"And that's how I turned you into a single father."

"You certainly did. I'm glad Gram and Gramps were around to help me out at first. I didn't know a thing about babies. I guess you could say we've grown up together."

"Know what? I wish I could remember my mommy, your sister."

"Well, know what, Mark? I remember her very well. After all, she and I grew up together."

"Will you tell me all about her again?"

"Yes, indeed I will. Go get the photo album from the bookcase, bottom shelf, and we'll begin—again."

*T*ell me, Mom, how you became my *now* mom."

"A student at my school was going to have a baby. Mary and her boyfriend decided that they were too young to care for a baby properly. They felt that someone who was older and ready, someone who wanted a child more than anything, should adopt their baby. They wanted to choose your new mother themselves."

"So they picked you?"

"Yes, lucky me."

"And it didn't matter to them that you weren't married, that you'd be a single parent?"

"Not a bit. What mattered was that I was a loving, caring person. So we made the arrangements and we all signed papers, and then the time came for you to be born.

"I got the phone call from Mary's mother just as I came in the door from work. I was supposed to go to dinner with Aunt Anne to celebrate my birthday, but I left a message for her and dashed right back out and drove to the hospital.

"I held Mary's hand—your birth mother's hand—and we both cried together when you came out of her body. Suddenly I had a daughter whose birthday was the same day as mine!

"Your birth parents spent the next day loving you and saying good-bye. Then I came back to pick you up. I dressed you in a rosebud sleeper and matching bunting. When we got home, our family and friends were here with food and gifts and a huge WELCOME HOME, OLIVIA sign."

"Tell me the part about my name again."

"I had asked Mary what she would name you, and she said, 'Oliver if the baby's a boy, and Olivia if it's a girl.' I kept the name she chose for you."

"And then my birth mother moved to California. But you still keep in touch and tell her about me, right?"

"And thank her, every day of my life."

D ad, tell me how we got to be father and son."
"Sure. Your mother and I were celebrating Kwanzaa—"
"Which night?"
"The fifth night, *Nia*."
"That means 'Purpose.' "

"Now hang on a second. Who's telling this story, anyway? As I was saying, we had just celebrated *Nia* and were leaving the building when we ran into the Davises and their newborn girl, Samantha. Your mother 'oohed' and 'aahed' so over that child."

"Just Mommy?"

"Well, I've got to admit I did my share, too."

"So, on the way home, you said to Mommy, 'Speaking of purpose...'"

"That's exactly what I said, and right then and there we decided that it was time."

"And you didn't change your minds?"

"Are you kidding? Mommy went to Dr. Lewis the very next week and told her how we felt about adopting. It turned out that Dr. Lewis had another patient who was pregnant, who felt she was too young and too poor to keep her child. So she asked Dr. Lewis to help her find a family for her baby when it was born. Once we found that out, the waiting was hard."

"But it was only six months, right, Dad?"

"Yes, only six months till we got the most important news of our lives."

"The news that I was born."

"Exactly."

"And you were lucky to find me so fast because some people wait years and years for a child."

"I guess that proves we were made for each other, huh?"

"Uh-*huh*. And you and Mommy named me 'Habib' because it means...what does it mean again, Dad?"

"It means 'beloved.' Absolutely beloved."

*T*ell me, Daddy, about how you got your girl."

"Even though we had three children, we knew our family wasn't finished yet."

"Because it was waiting for just the right person."

"Yes. We searched through the Blue Books, where children who need new homes are pictured. When we saw you, we looked into adopting you.

"We found out that you had lived with your birth mother for two months. Then two foster families cared for you after that. We decided that our home would be your only home from then on."

"For always, period. But I was shy at first, remember?"

"How could I forget? The first time we visited, we left without even really seeing you! You held Ellie, your elephant toy, in front of your face the entire time."

"But I got over that, finally."

"And then the big day came. We picked you up—all of us— in our new van, loaded you and your wheelchair on, and started back on the long ride home."

"You had three sons. Now me."

"I kept thinking how beautifully black braids went with blond buzz cuts as I looked at all my children. Pretty soon your brown eyes hooked into your brothers' blue, and you all began bickering over whose ice cream cone was biggest and whose singing voice was best, as brothers and sisters do.

"You came to us already named Nicole, already talking and done with kindergarten, your baby days behind you. We had a lot of catching up to do, but that was all right because we'd have a lot of time together."

"We've got forever, right, Daddy?"

"Right."

"And that's the end of the story."

"Oh, Nicole, that's just the beginning!"